Ciaran Murtagh is a writer of books and television programmes for children. Ciaran lives in London — to find out more about what he's writing and appearing in, follow him on Twitter @ciaranmurtagh or head over to www.ciaranmurtagh.com

Books by Ciaran Murtagh

CHARLIE FLINT AND THE DINOS

Dinopants

Dinopoo

Dinoburps

Dinoball

BALTHAZAR THE GENIE

Genie in Training

Genie in Trouble

Genie in a Trap

THE FINCREDIBLE DIARY OF FIN SPENCER

Stuntboy

Megastar

STUNTBOY
THE FINCREDIBLE DIARY OF FIN SPENCER

by CIARAN MURTAGH

with illustrations throughout by TIM WESSON

Piccadilly
PRESS

First published in Great Britain in 2015
by Piccadilly Press
Northburgh House, 10 Northburgh Street, London EC1V 0AT
www.piccadillypress.co.uk

Text copyright © Ciaran Murtagh, 2015
Illustrations copyright © Tim Wesson, 2015

A CIP catalogue record for this book is available from the British Library.

ISBN: 978-1-84812-434-9

5 7 9 10 8 6

Text design: Mina Bach
Printed and bound by Clays Ltd, St Ives Plc

Piccadilly Press is part of the Bonnier Publishing Group
www.bonnier.com

To the real Finn and Ellie,
from Dad

SUNDAY

Let's get this straight – I am **NOT** a diary person! Never have been, never will be. I've never worn a cardigan, never collected a stamp, never eaten salad and never had a nosebleed on the high board in a swimming pool. Okay, there was that one time, but that was only because I slipped and headbutted the safety rail. (WHY CALL IT A SAFETY RAIL WHEN IT'S OBVIOUSLY SO DANGEROUS?)

I'm more your stuntboy by day, rockstar by night kind of person. Or at least I will be when I stop being twelve years old. Until then I do what I can . . .

This is me, by the way —

FIN SPENCER.

I'm about to set a new world record for stunt-jumping. Almost. Well everybody's got to start somewhere, right? The girl's my six-year-old sister, **ELLIE**.

She's as annoying as a homemade
birthday present from your grandma.

Now, I know what you're thinking.
You're thinking,

Fin, you're obviously one super cool dude,
far too cool to own a diary,
let alone write one.
WHAT ARE YOU DOING?

Well the truth is, I didn't want this diary.
It was given to me by a batty old lady at a
funfair. I'll tell you about that in a minute.
I was going to throw the diary in the bin
straight away, when I had a brilliant idea . . .

EVERYONE loves reading about celebrities,
don't they? Footballers, actors, pop stars

— they all write about themselves and make a fortune. One day I'm going to be the most famous person on the planet. And when that happens, people are going to want to read all about me, too. This diary is my ticket to future millions! Cool, huh?

In a couple of weeks there's a school talent show and I'll get my very first taste of fame when I win. This diary will show future fans how I did it. I can already hear the cash tills ringing – **Kerching!**

Now, before we get onto that, let me tell you about the batty old lady at the funfair.

The reason I was at the funfair today was to ride **THE EXTERMINATOR**. Everyone knows The Exterminator is the most terrifying ride ever created. It's the perfect ride for a wannabe stuntboy like me. The only problem was I'd been grounded for a week for showing my sister my best wrestling move. (You'd think she'd want to learn.) Anyway, **ELLIE** had been bugging Mum and Dad to let her go to the funfair too and they were too busy to take her. Apparently there were loads of household chores that just had to be done — Dad was actually doing the washing for once.

So I decided to try and get back into their good books — and get myself to the funfair — by offering to take **ELLIE**. It worked perfectly. Before I was allowed out of the house, though, I had to listen to a whole ten minutes of **DAD RULES**. He's got a rule for everything!

We eventually got to the fair but as soon as **ELLIE** saw The Exterminator she started moaning she didn't like it. So I told her to wait in a spot where I could see her and promised to take her to her favourite ride in a minute.

When I finally got to the front of the queue for The Exterminator there was a sign sticking out of the ground with a red line showing how tall you had to be and

I was shorter than the line. The spotty freak in charge of the ride just looked at me and shook his head. I did my best to persuade him, but nothing worked. Then, to make

matters worse, **BRAD RADLEY** walked past and got straight on. Brad and his mates think they're really cool, but **BRAD**'s actually the meanest kid in school.

By the time I got back to **ELLIE** she had started to cry so I did the one thing I knew would keep her quiet and I took her to the UNiCORN iSLaND ride. But the spotty freak in charge of that wouldn't let **ELLIE** on by herself. Apparently adults have to ride with little kids — but he'd count me as an adult because he was nice like that . . .

NO WAY!

We were going home.

But then **ELLIE** started to cry even harder. The only reason I'd been allowed to come to the funfair in the first place was so that **ELLIE** could go to UNICORN ISLAND, and she

couldn't unless I went too and if I refused I knew she'd tell Mum and Dad and then I'd be grounded forever. Or at least until Tuesday. I had no choice — I got on the ride.

Just as the ride started, **BRAD RADLEY** spotted me. He laughed, took out his phone and snapped a picture.

I was so embarrassed I wanted to ram the unicorn's horn through my eyeball.

I was in such a bad mood that when the ride stopped I leaped off the thing like Batman and marched **ELLIE** towards the exit. We were about to leave when the batty old lady I mentioned before popped out of her tent and stood in our way. She looked like she was over a hundred years old. She said,

Come into my tent and I'll tell you your future.

I felt like telling her I already know my future, Grandma — getting ripped at school tomorrow for riding on a unicorn with my kid sister!

Before I could say anything, **ELLIE** and the old lady were inside the tent. I wanted to leave her there, but then I couldn't really leave my kid sister alone with a stranger, and believe me, they didn't come stranger than this lady. I followed them inside.

The old lady asked me if I was enjoying the funfair.

'**NO**,' I said. 'In fact, it shouldn't be called

a funfair at all. It should be called an un-funfair.' And then for some reason I told her what had happened. 'I really wish I could change a few things,' I said as I finished.

She nodded and smiled in that way old ladies do. Then she gave me this diary and said,

This might help you get what you want.

How's a diary going to help me get what I want? Doesn't she know that diaries are for dweebs and losers? I am neither, thank you very much! I needed to get out of there before the batty old bat could give me something else I didn't need, like a chocolate teapot or a lifetime's supply of beard shavings. I snatched the diary, said thank you — even though I didn't mean it — and yanked **ELLIE** out of the tent.

As we hurried home, all I could think about was how **BRAD RADLEY** and his stupid camera phone were going to ruin my life before it had even started.

MONDAY

Today was the worst day of my life. SERIOUSLY. THE. WORST. DAY. EVER. A day so bad I wish I'd just stayed in bed.

Things went wrong as soon as I got up. Remember I said that Dad did the washing yesterday, for just about the first time ever?

It turns out there's a reason Dad doesn't normally do the washing — IT'S BECAUSE HE'S NO GOOD AT IT!

He dyed all of my school shirts pink! Not just any pink either, but BRIGHT PINK. Stayed-out-in-the-sun-until-your-nostrils-bleed pink. Then I tried on my trousers. Disaster! He'd boil-washed them and they

were smaller than a **hamster's bikini.**

Then the penny dropped. No school uniform meant no school! **Result!** Maybe the day wasn't going to be a total washout after all. **WASHOUT**. Get it? (Did I mention I'm a comedian, too?).

Anyway, I ditched the school uniform and pulled on some jeans and a T-shirt.

When Mum saw what I was wearing she nearly blew her top. Then I explained it was all Dad's fault so she blew her top at him instead. Double result!

Dad tried to lighten the mood by showing us all this lame cartoon from the paper called 'Kids Say the Sweetest Things'. He thinks it's hysterical but anyone with half a brain knows it's cringier than a four-year-old's birthday party. This was the cringiest yet. It was a picture of a little old man and a snot-nosed kid. The snot-nosed kid was pointing at the little old man and asking, 'WHY IS YOUR FACE SO WRINKLY? DID YOU STAY IN THE BATH TOO LONG?'

Dad laughed and laughed and then Mum joined in. Sometimes I worry about my parents. No, scratch that — I <u>always</u> worry about my parents.

I was about to explain why it was so bad when I spotted something on the opposite page. It was an advert for the coolest rock band in the world, **X-WING**. It turns out they're playing in town next week! I have to go.

I was looking at the advert when **ELLIE** spotted one for her favourite singer, ChaRLIE DIMPLES, on the same page. He's playing next week too. Ugh. He's cringier than the 'Kids Say the Sweetest Things' cartoon and a four-year-old's birthday party COMBINED.

I pointed at the paper and asked if I could go to the concert. Mum and Dad were still too busy chuckling at the cartoon to pay much attention, but Mum wiped away a tear and said, 'We'll see!', which we all know is mum-speak for 'Definitely'. Triple result!

I poured myself a bowl of Coco Snaps, grabbed the remote and settled down for a long hard day of cartoon-watching. My bum had barely brushed the sofa when Mum hauled me up and marched me upstairs, saying she was sure my uniform wasn't as bad as I said it was. She made me try on everything again and then stood back to have a look.

'It's not that bad,' she said.

NOT **BAD?**

NOT BAD?!

It was worse than the last dessert on the canteen counter. I looked like I was starring in a film called:

She couldn't make me go to school like that! Could she?

It turned out she could.

The only person who didn't laugh when I got to school was **JOSH DOYLE**. **JOSH** is my best friend. I've known him since I was three — we've been through **A LOT** together.

We're performing a double act in the talent show next week. We had a bit of an argument about what we're doing. It got so bad we nearly stopped being best friends. I wanted to jump over him on my bike, but he was worried that he might get squashed. Which was a fair point — he might get squashed. But if you can't squash your best friend, then who can you squash? **JOSH** wanted to tell some jokes. But **JOSH** doesn't know any funny jokes and the ones I know you can't tell at school. In the end we decided that I'd jump over a shark tank while he played a solo on his guitar. Not a tank of real sharks, obviously. Dad got me a wind-up shark as a joke present last Christmas. It's really lame, but it can keep going for absolutely ages. I'm putting it in an old fish tank and jumping over it while it's swimming about in there. **FUNNY, DANGEROUS, COOL!** We're going to win easily!

Anyway, back to this morning. When **JOSH** saw what I was wearing he put his arm around me and said,

You look RIDICULOUS.

You can always rely on **JOSH** to tell the truth, even when he should probably lie his head off.

Still at least the day couldn't get any worse, right?

WRONG.

At break time a group of kids gathered around the noticeboard. **JOSH** and I made our way to the front to see what all the fuss was about. When I saw what was pinned to the board I wanted to hug a hedgehog. There was a mocked-up poster with a photo of me riding the unicorn. The caption underneath read, I'VE been to Unicorn Island.

I tore down the poster, but it was too late — everyone had seen it. Wherever I went people kept saying, 'How was Unicorn Island, **FIN**?'

At least now the day couldn't get any worse, right?

WRONG!

I'd forgotten that after break it was gym. I don't mind gym. Sure, Mr Bucklestrap the gym teacher is a maniac, but that's part of his job.

It was only when I was walking into the changing room that I realised I had a major problem. I'd been so worried about what I was going to wear to school that morning that I'd <u>forgotten to bring in my gym kit</u>. But then I realised it was probably just as well. Who knew what Dad had turned my gym kit into in his magic washing machine?

I hid in the changing room and hoped that Mr Bucklestrap wouldn't notice.

No such luck.

When he barged in I went through my usual list of excuses.

At first it looked like Mr Bucklestrap was going to be understanding for once. But then he said two of the most terrifying words in the English language:

LOST PROPERTY.

He pointed at a heap of clothes that I swear have been sitting in the corner since 1982.

I shuddered. He couldn't make me wear those! Could he?

It turned out he could. The best T-shirt I could find stank of cheesy feet, and the elastic had snapped in the running shorts.

Still, at least I could rely on my best buddy **JOSH** to cheer me up.

You look RIDICULOUS.

he said.

Thanks, **JOSH**. I'm really starting to think I need a better best friend.

I spent the rest of the gym lesson in the corner, stinking of cheese and holding up my shorts. I wanted to be as far away from the basketball as possible. But **BRAD RADLEY** saw what I was up to and chucked the ball at my face. I couldn't risk damaging my rock-star good looks so I let go of the shorts to catch the ball and they ended up around my ankles.

The whole class stared at me and then started laughing. I didn't blame them. I was

standing in the gym IN MY PANTS.
I'D STARE AND THEN I'D LAUGH TOO.

Mr Bucklestrap saw me and yelled so hard I thought his head was going to pop.

I pulled up my shorts and sloped off while everyone else finished the game. When the lesson was over, Mr Bucklestrap had a go at me again for forgetting my kit and parading my pants in public.

I tried to explain that none of this was my fault, but Mr Bucklestrap wasn't listening so I got a detention anyway.

For the rest of the day I was sure I stank of **LOST PROPERTY**. No matter what I did I couldn't seem to get rid of the smell of cheesy feet.

School could not finish soon enough! Then,

just as I was on my way to detention, **BRAD RADLEY** cornered me in the corridor. He whipped out his phone again and took a picture of me in my pink-and-tiny uniform. 'To remind me of what a dweeb looks like,' he said. He laughed as he announced to me and everyone else in the corridor what I'd done. He said I was only allowed on baby rides at the fair, I loved to wear pink, I showed everybody in the class my pants and I stank of cheesy feet. When he'd finished he looked me up and down and pointed saying,

Look, it's
FINTERRIBLE FIN!

A laugh went up behind me and all of a sudden I realised he'd just invented a new nickname. **FINTERRIBLE FIN**.

Brilliant. **BRAD RADLEY** might be a mean kid, but I've got to admit he is sharp.

For once, detention with Mr Bucklestrap seemed like a relief.

After I was released, I was out of the school gates faster than a jet-pack javelin! When I got home, Mum had been to the shops and bought me a new uniform. She made me spaghetti on toast for tea and made the spaghetti into a smiley face.

Even that didn't cheer me up.

I decided to come up here and write down my miserable day in this diary. Sometimes getting it all off your chest makes you feel better, right? **WRONG!**

If anything, seeing it all written down made me feel a million times worse. I suppose, even the most famous celebrities have bad days, every now and then. The time Lewis Hamilton stubbed his toe on a Ferrari, the day Simon Cowell farted in his Jacuzzi . . . that sort of thing. Well, I owe it to my future fans to tell them EVERTHING — no matter how painful.

That didn't stop me hating **BRAD RADLEY** and his stupid phone though. Someone needs to stand up to him. I wish I'd just told him that he's nothing but a big bully and lots of people think so but they're just too scared to say anything. If anyone's terrible it's him.

I'm not finterrible, I'm fincredible — **FINCREDIBLE FIN SPENCER.** That's what I want to be known as — and I will be when **JOSH** and I win the talent show with our stuntboy—rockstar act!

TUESDAY

If yesterday was **THE WORST DAY EVER**, today was the **weirdest**. Weirder than a chocolate-covered chinchilla. And I have a sneaking suspicion that writing things down here might have had something to do with it. But we'll get on to that, for now, let's start at the beginning.

I wasn't looking forward to going to school. Would you, if your new nickname was

FINTERRIBLE FIN? Everywhere I went I knew it would be '**FINTERRIBLE**' this and '**FINTERRIBLE**' that. I pretended to be ill so that Mum would let me stay at home.

No such luck. Mum saw right through it, of course — she always does. I think she might be psychic or something.

Anyway, I got my nice new uniform out of the wardrobe and pulled it on. It was itchier than a nit's armpit, but at least it wasn't PINK. I headed downstairs for breakfast. It wasn't a good start — **ELLIE** had eaten all the Coco Snaps so Mum made me eat some of her special Keep Fit breakfast cereal. It tastes like cardboard and turns your poo into house bricks.

When I got to school I was already in a bad mood — and that was before people started calling me **FINTERRIBLE FIN**, like I knew they were going to.

But here's the weird thing . . .

As I walked down the corridor everyone was looking at me. Not a surprise, after the day I'd had yesterday.

But then I noticed they were looking at me in a (GOOD) way. Now that was a surprise! And the strangest thing of all was when **CLAUDIA RONSON**, the prettiest girl

in my class, came right up to me and said, 'What you did yesterday, **FIN**, was fincredible!'

Fincredible? Did I just hear her right? What did I do yesterday other than make a complete fool of myself? Maybe that's what she goes for. If so, I wished I'd known sooner – I'd have done it ages ago!

Then one of **CLAUDIA**'s friends started clapping, and before I knew it, lots of people were clapping. Did they like my pants that much? I could tell them where to buy some for themselves — they were 'buy one get one free' in the supermarket.

The attention freaked me out so much that by the time I got to my locker I was a nervous wreck and I dropped my key on the floor. Before I could pick it up, **BRAD RADLEY** was on his hands and knees picking it up for me.

This had to be some sort of trick, right? He was going to hold the key up in front of everyone and say, 'I've found the key to being Finterrible and it belongs to Fin Spencer!' or something like that. He may like making me feel bad, but he can be quite funny sometimes.

But he didn't say anything of the sort. He just smiled, helped me to open my locker and then he started to fill my rucksack with books. Something VERY ODD was going on. Maybe **BRAD** had fallen over, bumped his head and woken up as a COMPLETELY DIFFERENT PERSON!

As he put my chemistry book into my bag, he started to apologise for all the things he'd

41

said yesterday. **BRAD RADLEY**! Apologising! I was so shocked ants could have been tap-dancing on my forehead and I wouldn't have noticed! Apparently Brad had been thinking it over and he'd realised I was right — everything I'd said had really hit home.

HANG ON! EVERYTHING I'D SAID? But I hadn't said <u>ANYTHING</u> yesterday. He'd made me look like a dweeb and I'd just stood there and said nothing — like a dweeb!

As I was going over all this in my head he was still talking. He was saying that he knew he shouldn't be such a big bully, and then he announced that he'd decided to turn over a new leaf starting right now. From this day on, **BRAD RADLEY** was going to be nice to everyone. Then he threw an arm around my

42

shoulder and gave me a big hug. 'You're **FINCREDIBLE FIN**,' he said.

I blinked in disbelief at what had just happened. Then **JOSH** came up to me, smiling from ear to ear. He leaned in close and said, 'Well done, mate — you were **FINCREDIBLE** yesterday.'

Now I can take **CLAUDIA RONSON** telling me I'm her number one guy. (Okay, she didn't QUITE say that but it was close.) I can even take **BRAD RADLEY** giving me a hug. But **JOSH** calling me fincredible because of what happened yesterday? That's just crazy! I hadn't done ANYTHING. I marched **JOSH** into the boys' toilets and demanded to know what was going on.

He seemed a bit confused. 'You know,

yesterday, when you finally stood up to **BRAD RADLEY**!'

When I did <u>WHAT</u>? 'Go on,' I said. 'It's all a bit of a blur to me, for some reason.'

'You've got to remember! He was taking the mickey out of you for all those daft things you did — the uniform, the pants, the cheesy stink, the Unicorn Island thing . . .'

Yes, yes, yes! Get on with it! I thought.

'But instead of just standing there, you told him that he was nothing but a big bully and lots of people thought so. Then you told him you weren't finterrible, you were fincredible — **FINCREDIBLE FIN SPENCER** — and you'd prove it by winning the talent show with me next week.'

WHAT WAS HE TALKING ABOUT?

Had the caretaker pumped the corridor full of crazy gas or something? That's not what I remembered at all. It's what I wished I had said but that's a very different thing. I'd NEVER dare say that to BRAD RADLEY's face.

Before I could say anything, JOSH took out his phone and played a video of me telling BRAD exactly what I, and everyone else, thought of him. (It seems like everyone's got a fantastic camera phone which can take really great videos except me. I haven't got any kind of phone, not even one that makes calls. I don't want to make calls, but I do want to take photos and videos and surf the 'net and . . . well EVERYTHING! But guess what? A phone is first prize in the school talent show, so it's only a matter of time.)

Anyway, back to the video on **JOSH**'s phone. It was definitely ME, telling **BRAD RADLEY** exactly what I thought of him. So why couldn't I remember saying any of it? Suddenly it dawned on me — I was obviously still fast asleep and dreaming. I needed to wake up.

I asked **JOSH** to pinch me, which he was a little too happy to do, if you ask me.

It hurt, but I didn't wake up.

Then I realised that what everyone thought I'd said was exactly what I'd written in my diary. I was about to tell **JOSH** this when the bell rang.

In class Mrs Johnson gave us a maths test

and I was brought back to reality with a bump. It's not that I'm bad at maths . . . IT'S THAT I'M TERRIBLE AT MATHS!

$$2+2 = 22 \qquad 1+1 = 11$$

She mentioned it yesterday, but I must have been so distracted by everything that I forgot all about it. I had meant to get up early this morning and revise for it but even though I always mean to, I NEVER DO. This time, if I had actually got up and revised, I know I could have done well — it was quite easy for a maths test. I did my best. I knew I'd got at least one question right . . .

TEST PAPER

QUESTION 1

NAME: Fin Spencer ✓

But that was a small blip in an amazing day! Because I'd apparently stood up to **BRAD**, quite a lot of people were super nice to me. In the lunch hall there's a special table next to the window where **BRAD RADLEY** and the cool kids sit. I NEVER sit there. Today they asked me to join them.

BRAD RADLEY even went to get my lunch for me and shared his crisps. Maybe I've misjudged him. I always knew he could be mean, but he can be pretty funny too. Now that we've had our little chat we might even become friends.

Days like today just don't happen to me. I was the centre of attention. I was a hero. I was incredible. No, scratch that — I was **FINCREDIBLE**!

As I was heading back to class after lunch, **CLAUDIA RONSON** came over for the second time and said, 'Hi!'

I was so nervous I didn't know what to say back. It was as if my mouth had gone to Mars. I just smiled like a dweeb and scurried into class. If I really was **FINCREDIBLE FIN** I'd have said something funny or clever immediately, wouldn't I? But my brain doesn't work like that. OH WELL! Days can't be completely perfect, can they?

When I got home, I sat in my room and got out this diary. Something strange was going on and I wondered if this diary was behind it. I leafed back through the pages. Yesterday I wrote what I wanted to say to **BRAD** and today everybody thought that was what I really had said, even if I knew I hadn't. Yesterday I wanted to be **FINCREDIBLE FIN SPENCER** and today I AM. Is this diary magic?

NOW HOLD ON! I know that magic diaries don't exist. If I start telling people I've got a magic diary they might think I really did go to UNICORN Island and that they made me king while I was there.

I don't want to think about it too much, because whatever's going on, today was THE BEST DAY EVER — apart from the maths test and looking like a dweeb in front of **CLAUDIA RONSON**. I really should have got up a bit earlier this morning and revised, and I really wish I'd said something cool back to **CLAUDIA** — something like, 'Hi! Fincredible Fin speaking!' — and given her a wink and a cheeky smile.

TOO LATE NOW. But there's always tomorrow. And who knows, now that I've written it in the diary maybe it'll work its magic again. Not that I really believe in magic, of course, but . . . well anything's possible when you're **FINCREDIBLE**.

WEDNESDAY

When I woke up this morning I couldn't wait to get to school. I knew that school was going to be **SOOOOO MUCH COOLER** now I was Fincredible! I hopped out of bed and rushed downstairs for breakfast.

While I was sitting at the table Mum put her hand on my forehead and asked if I was feeling all right.

I told her I'd never felt better and then both my mum and dad shared a worried look. Apparently they'd never seen me looking so cheerful in the morning and they thought I might be coming down with something. Typical! Yesterday I spent all morning trying to convince them that I was ill and today, when I was feeling fine, they thought I'd got pneumonia or something. PARENTS! How do they get it so wrong? You'd think they'd *be better* at it by now; they've had TWELVE YEARS of practice!

Anyway, nothing was going to spoil my mood, not even Mum telling me she'd decided to stop buying Coco Snaps. She thought we should all eat her disgusting Keep Fit cereal every day instead. 'It will keep you regular,' she said. That's mum-speak for 'Make you poo lots'. Mums are obsessed with things like that. Don't ask me why. You'd think they'd have better things to do with their time — like BUYING COCO SNAPS! ⟵——

Anyway, as I said, I wasn't going to let it get me down. Today was going to be awesome.

As I was walking through the school gates I waved to all my new friends (or should that be fans?). Then I spotted **CLAUDIA RONSON** and strolled over to say hello. I was trying to be cool, to make up for yesterday, but she just acted like I was 𝚒𝚗𝚟𝚒𝚜𝚒𝚋𝚕𝚎 or something.

That was weird. I know I couldn't think of anything to say to her yesterday, but surely that didn't mean she'd ignore me COMPLETELY today?

I told **JOSH** what had happened with **CLAUDIA** when we were lining up for registration. He said he had overheard **CLAUDIA** tell her mates that she thought I was a bighead because yesterday I'd told her I was **FINCREDIBLE FIN** and then I'd winked and given her this really creepy smile, like I was farting or something.

What was **JOSH** talking about? I've barely forgiven him for not letting me stunt-jump over him at the talent show and now he's saying **CLAUDIA** thinks I'm creepy? He needs to watch out — there are other people to be friends with. Anyway, I didn't smile at her at all, I just walked off embarrassed.

It was then that I knew for sure just how amazing this diary is. It DOES make things happen — it IS magic!

Last night I definitely wrote that I wished I'd said something cool to **CLAUDIA** and given her a cheeky smile. And now it seems like that's what I did! Well, it may have backfired a bit — **CLAUDIA** wasn't impressed by me calling myself fincredible, and she thought my cheeky smile was creepy — but that's not the point. The point is,

THIS DIARY IS MAGIC

Now that I was sure, I knew the rest of the day was going to be a breeze.

I practically skipped into Mrs Johnson's class. She looked me up and down and asked if I was feeling all right. Honestly! A grown-up wouldn't know a sick kid if they coughed up a lung in their face.

Once everyone was sitting down Mrs Johnson handed back the tests from yesterday. At first I was a bit scared to look at it. But then I remembered that if I was right about the diary, I had nothing to worry about!

I flipped over the paper and, sure enough, I'd done brilliantly! It was the first time that had ever happened! It was so rare, Mrs Johnson asked me to stand up while the whole class gave me a round of applause. OKAY, THAT WAS SLIGHTLY EMBARRASSING, BUT I COULD COPE WITH IT. Then she gave me three merits and said she'd send an email home to my parents.

The rest of the morning sailed by.

+ A

As I was going off to lunch I gave Mrs Johnson my cheeky smile. She asked me if I needed to go to the toilet . . .

After lunch **BRAD RADLEY** came over to me and **JOSH** in the playground and showed us some really cool videos on his phone. **BRAD** and me were laughing like drains but **JOSH** wasn't. He just looked at us and said,

I don't get it.

JOSH has never been the smartest meerkat in the burrow, and now he's starting to be <u>EMBARRASSING</u> too. **JOSH** has been my best friend forever, but recently he's been a bit dweeby. He ruined my idea for the best talent show stunt ever, he told me that my smile is creepy and now he won't laugh at videos that are really funny. I'm starting to think that he might be the dweeby best friend that dweeby Fin deserved. But I'm not dweeby Fin any more, I'm **FINCREDIBLE FIN**, and **FINCREDIBLE FIN** deserves a fincredible best mate. Someone like **BRAD RADLEY**.

BRAD can be mean and rude, but if the joke's not on you he can also be really funny. Truth be told, I've always kind of wished **BRAD** was on my side, and that we were mates. **BRAD RADLEY** might be a dweeb's arch-enemy, but he's a fincredible kid's best friend!

When the bell rang for the end of lunch, **JOSH** ran into school, like the dweeb he is, while **BRAD** and I took our time. As we were walking, **BRAD** asked me what I was doing for the talent show. I told him what **JOSH** and I had decided — I was going to jump over a shark tank on a bike while **JOSH** played a guitar solo.

When **BRAD** heard my plans he said it sounded like the coolest stunt in the history of cool stunts and I told him he wasn't wrong. I can nearly do it, too. I can ride a bike, I've got a wind-up shark, I can even jump over stuff. Now I just need to pull it all together. HOW HARD CAN IT BE?

As we walked across the playground, **BRAD** said he had just one question: could I trust **JOSH** not to muck everything up? And as we were making our way into class that question started to play in my head. I knew I'd be fine

— but **JOSH** was a liability. **JOSH** was ALWAYS a liability, especially in front of hundreds of people. I have to make sure **JOSH** isn't going to let me down. We are going to practise like we've never practised before.

When I got home Mum was waiting for me in the hall with a printout of Mrs Johnson's email. She gave me a big hug and told me how proud she was and that there was a surprise for me on the kitchen table.

I ran to take a look and there I saw . . .

A BIG BOX OF COCO SNAPS!

Okay, it wasn't the ticket to the **X-WING** concert I was hoping for, but it was a start. And that gave me an idea . . .

The paper was still on the table so I opened it at the page of adverts and said, 'THAT is going to be a great concert.'

Mum actually looked at the page, raised an eyebrow and said, 'We'll see.' Which everybody knows is mum-speak for 'I'll call up the band and get backstage passes!' Those tickets are in the bag!

After dinner I rushed upstairs, and just before I started writing, I gave the diary a kiss. I might kiss it again when I've finished! It deserves all the love I can give it. That batty old lady at the funfair was right. This diary can get me anything I want! Sure, things aren't great with **CLAUDIA**, but that's not the diary's fault — that was mine for not thinking it through properly. I'll get it right next time.

This diary lets me change history. I can do or say anything I want and it doesn't matter — I can just use the diary to make it better! I'M UNTOUCHABLE!

Bring on tomorrow — I'm going to have FUN!

THURSDAY

Ever had one of those days where you know nothing can go wrong? I have, and it was all thanks to my Fincredible Diary!

The fun started at breakfast. As I came downstairs **ELLIE** was about to help herself to my Coco Snaps, the Coco Snaps Mum had bought me for doing so well at school yesterday. That wasn't fair and for once Mum actually agreed with me. She made Ellie hand the box over and told her that she could have some after I'd eaten my fill. I like a challenge, so I ate seventeen bowls of Coco Snaps one after the other. It took half an hour and made my eyes go funny, but it was worth it.

By the time I'd finished there were no Coco Snaps left. Result! **ELLIE** had to eat Keep Fit breakfast cereal instead. Double result! Mum was really cross when she saw what had happened. I shrugged and belched, 'Sorry', but I was laughing so much I fell off the chair.

That made Mum even crosser, but WHO CARES? This diary is going to make sure nobody but me remembers anything about it tomorrow!

When I got to school I changed into an **X-WING** T-shirt and trainers I'd brought from home. As I walked down the corridor everybody stared. I was getting used to that now. They couldn't believe what I was doing, but **FINCREDIBLE FIN** had decided that uniforms were for dweebs, **X-WING** T-shirts were for <u>WINNERS</u>.

When **CLAUDIA** saw me she turned away and whispered to her friends. I knew she'd be impressed.

BRAD met me at my locker and helped me with my books again. As he was packing my rucksack, **JOSH** arrived.

He seemed really worried.

You look RIDICULOUS.

he said.

JOSH is soooo boring. I did not look ridiculous — I looked fincredible. **BRAD** said he thought I looked amazing — that's more like it! It's obvious **JOSH** and I are drifting apart. It's not a problem though — now **BRAD**'s not being mean to me I like him, and he's got cool friends so now I don't have to hang around with **JOSH** all the time.

At registration Mrs Johnson asked me what I thought I was wearing. I told her, 'I don't think I'm wearing anything, I KNOW I'm wearing an **X-WING** T-shirt.' I'd never normally have dared to say anything like that, but knowing I could change whatever was going to happen by writing in my diary made me feel invincible.

The class started to laugh. Mrs Johnson gave me a look and asked what had happened to my uniform. I told her a badger ate it.

The class laughed even louder and Mrs Johnson started to fume. I could almost see smoke coming out of her ears. She asked if I was feeling all right. **NOT AGAIN** — I felt

FINE! I asked her if she was feeling all right because she was the one with smoke coming out of her ears. Then I winked at **CLAUDIA** and she shook her head in disbelief.

When the class had stopped laughing Mrs Johnson said, 'We can discuss your uniform choices at break time.' Which everybody knows is teacher-speak for 'You're in big trouble.' It doesn't matter though — thanks to this diary, tomorrow she won't remember any of it and I'll be back in her good books.

In English Mrs Houstoun announced a surprise spelling test. One by one we had to stand up and spell a word that she chose. I've never seen the point of spelling. HAVE TEACHERS NOT HEARD OF AUTOCORRECT?

Anyway, when she got to me she picked a really hard one. I bet it was on purpose. She asked me to spell 'uranium'. I stood up and began, 'U . . . R . . . A . . .' And then a fincredible idea popped into my head. I turned to **JOSH** and said, 'U . . . R . . . A . . . Dweeb!'

Everyone started to laugh again — apart from **JOSH** and Mrs Houstoun. If I'm being honest, I felt a bit bad for making fun of **JOSH** in front of everybody. But then, he is being a bit of a dweeb at the moment. He's always got a reason why I shouldn't do something instead of a reason why I should. Besides, it was funny and, thanks to this diary, everyone will have forgotten about it by tomorrow so it doesn't really matter, DOES IT?

Mrs Johnson gave me a red docket. That meant I had to go to the headmaster after school. I've never had a red docket before — they're usually reserved for people like **BRAD RADLEY**. Then she also took back the three merits I got yesterday and made me sit outside the classroom until break. No more spelling test! Result!

After break (which I spent in Mrs Johnson's room "discussing my uniform choices") it was time for music. I LOVE MUSIC. I'm really good at it, too. The only problem is that Mr Burchester has terrible taste. He makes us play really `lame` stuff like nursery rhymes or songs from the 1970s, which no one ever remembers. Today he wanted us to play something called 'Stairway to Heaven' . . .

NEVER HEARD OF IT!

Couldn't he see I was wearing an**X-WING** T-shirt? That meant I was only going to play **X-WING**! I snatched up a guitar, cranked up the amp and let rip.

Mr Burchester shoved his fingers in his ears and unplugged the amp. <u>Spoilsport</u>. He made me play the xylophone instead. No problem — I can play **X-WING** on anything.

Then he took the xylophone away and gave me a triangle.

Then he took that away and made me sit in the corner sorting out sheet music for the school orchestra. I even managed to make that fun as I made paper aeroplanes out of the music and aimed them at Mr Burchester's head.

Then he gave me a red docket and I had to sit outside in the corridor until lunch. WHO CARES? Tomorrow he won't remember a thing either!

As we were lining up at lunch, **JOSH** came over and asked me what I was doing.

I told him I was having the best day ever. He told me I was being a total jerk. I said he was only feeling sore because I'd called him a dweeb in the spelling test. **JOSH** said that it wasn't just that, but everything I was doing was jerky.

I'd heard enough so I went and sat at the cool table where he wouldn't be allowed. **BRAD** shared his crisps with me again. Now I know **BRAD**'s got a heart of gold if you're on his side. He's a loyal friend, no matter what, unlike some people I could mention — **JOSH DOYLE**.

BRAD dared me to start a food fight in the canteen. EASY! In five seconds flat we were in the middle of beanageddon! In the saucy carnage **BRAD** and I managed to escape before the dinner ladies found us.

Then he dared me to write on the wall in the boys' toilets. At first I wasn't sure, but I didn't want **BRAD** to think I was a scaredy-cat, and besides, loads of people have written on the walls and have never been found out. I reckoned I'd have to be the unluckiest boy in the world to get caught.

It turned out I WAS THE UNLUCKIEST BOY IN THE WORLD. Mr Finch, the headmaster, came in just as I'd got my pen out. I started to make my usual excuses but Mr Finch wasn't listening. **BRAD** wasn't holding a pen, so he let him off with a warning.

I was about to say how unfair that was — I mean I hadn't even written anything! — when I remembered that none of this mattered anyway! Tomorrow this won't have happened.

I let Mr Finch drone on about how disappointed he was with me, how I'd already got two red dockets today and how an afternoon at home might 'Bring back the **FIN** we all know and love.' Which we all know is teacher-speak for 'You're usually a dweeb.'

It was only when he was marching me into his office that I realised he was going to call my parents. He asked for my mum's or dad's number and I gave him one of the numbers I know off by heart . . . It took him a few seconds to realise that Mama's Pizza and my mum are NOT the same person.

He stormed off to get the secretary to call home instead. As he was leaving he told me to have a think about what I'd done. And I did. I thought it was pretty cool! I'd had the courage to do all the things I'd always wanted to do, but had always been too scared to try. I wouldn't want to do them every day, but today, knowing that it was a one-off that everyone would forget, it was fun!

When Mum arrived at school she was embarrassed and very, <u>very</u> angry. She blamed my behaviour on the fact that I had eaten seventeen bowls of Coco Snaps that morning. She promised that she'd definitely never buy them again and that from now on I'd be eating Keep Fit cereal for breakfast EVERY MORNING.

When we got home Mum sent me straight up here to my room, shouting, 'If you think we'll be taking you to that concert after this then you've another think coming!'

BRILLIANT! I <u>knew</u> they'd got tickets! Now all I have to do is use the diary to put everything right and I'll still be on course for **X-WING** next week. I LOVE THIS DIARY. I just need to write it down, so here goes . . .

→ I want Mrs Johnson to forget ALL about the spelling test and give me back my merits — and of course I want **JOSH** to forget that I was ever mean to him (even though it was quite a good joke).

⟶ I want Mr Burchester to forget ALL about me misbehaving in music (and to make his next lesson an *X-WING* special).

⟶ I want the dinner ladies to forget about the food fight.

⟶ I want Mr Finch to forget he ever found me writing on the toilet wall.

⟶ In fact, I want EVERYBODY at school to forget all the naughty, show-offy things I did.

⟶ And I want Mum and Dad to forget everything about today and take me to the concert just like they'd planned.

There — that should do the trick. Tomorrow everything will be back to normal. I'll have had a great day today and no one will be any the wiser about what I got up to. I AM A GENIUS!

FRIDAY

I AM <u>NOT</u> A GENIUS.

As soon as I got downstairs this morning I knew something was wrong. My little sister was smiling at me as if I was in trouble.

| NORMAL FIN'S IN TROUBLE SMILE | SMALL 'FIN TROD IN DOG POO' SMILE | MEDIUM 'FIN BROKE A VASE' SMILE | BIG 'FIN BURNED THE HOUSE DOWN' SMILE |

Her smile was so big I knew I must be in the biggest trouble ever.

BUT I COULDN'T BE COULD I? This diary should have fixed everything right? No one should remember what I got up to yesterday. I changed it all. So maybe I was in trouble for something completely different that I didn't even know I'd done yet. That's what parents are like. Sometimes you never find out what they're really angry about.

I decided to pretend that I hadn't noticed **ELLIE**'s 'so big I'm going to eat my face' grin. Instead I flashed my own big smile at Mum and said, 'Good morning.'

Mum stared at me like I'd just used her wedding dress to clean the car and Dad grunted from behind the paper. **ELLIE**'s smile got even bigger, which I didn't think was possible. Seriously, it was like she was about to grin her own ears off or something.

Mum looked at me and started to list everything I did wrong yesterday. That was when I started to get <u>very worried</u>. She hadn't forgotten a thing, and when she said it out loud like that it sounded BAD.

WHY DIDN'T YOU WORK, DIARY?!

I poured myself a massive bowl of Keep Fit cereal and tried to change the subject.

I asked Dad about 'Kids Say the Sweetest Things'. He just grunted and turned the page. I really was in big trouble this time. I knew it right down to my spotty Spider-Man underpants.

Mum said she and Dad were going to have a chat about my behaviour after breakfast and then they'd decide on a 'suitable course of action'. Which everyone knows is Mum-speak for 'catapulted into space', or grounded at the very least.

Breakfast over, I ran out of the door and off to school. But it was only as I was turning into the school gates that I realised that if Mum and Dad hadn't forgotten what I did yesterday then nobody at school would have forgotten either. Suddenly I wanted to be whisked off to UNICORN ISLANd and live there forever — anything was better than walking through those gates!

Sure enough, when I got to school Mr Finch was waiting for me at the door. He took me straight to his office and made me apologise for everything. I had to go and see the dinner ladies and Mr Burchester and Mrs Houstoun to apologise. By the time I'd said 'I'm sorry' to each of them in turn I was starting to think my name was SORRY SPENCER.

And all this was before the day had even properly started! Mr Finch also handed me a list of punishments that I had to do at break time and lunchtime. BRILLIANT. I spent the whole of first class trying to be quieter than a human mouse to avoid getting into any more trouble.

And I spent first break scrubbing writing

off the toilet wall. It was so unfair. I didn't even get to make my own mark first! Normally **JOSH** would have helped me, but of course he hadn't forgotten how mean I'd been to him yesterday. When he saw me carrying the bucket and sponge down the corridor he just looked at me and mouthed the words

I told you so

in my direction.

Thanks, **JOSH**.

BRAD was far too cool to be seen washing toilet walls, which is fair enough I guess. He did invite me onto his table at lunch to make up for it but I was too busy picking up litter and sorting out the lost property pile. There's something about sorting through cheesy clothes that puts you <u>right off</u> your food . . .

By the time the bell rang at the end of the day, **FINCREDIBLE FIN** was a distant memory. Now I was a total loser.

Only **BRAD** seemed to think what I did yesterday was cool. I mean, even though he didn't help me with any of my punishments or anything, it was nice of him to say that and not rub my nose in it like **JOSH** did. It didn't really make me feel any better though. I mean, even I thought that all those things I did yesterday made me a total loser. I'd never, ever have done them if I had thought anyone was going to remember.

I'm glad it's almost the weekend. Maybe when I go back to school on Monday everyone will have forgotten.

I walked home on my own. When I got back **ELLIE** was still smiling, which meant I was still in trouble. Mum and Dad had decided to round off the perfect day by grounding me for THE WHOLE WEEKEND. At first I was angry, but then I remembered that nobody wanted to hang out with me anyway, so what did it matter?

I don't understand. I thought this diary would fix everything but it hasn't! It's made everything worse. I can't believe I thought I had a magic diary in the first place. I am a loser. I'm a loser for believing in magic diaries and listening to batty old ladies at funfairs. Whatever strange things have happened over the last couple of days must just be weird coincidences. I should have known. Fincredible things don't happen to a boy like me.

Anyway, all of this magic diary business has been very distracting but at least if I'm grounded I'll have lots of time to practise my stunt-jumping for the talent show next Friday. If I want to win the phone I need to be good. I hope **JOSH** is practising his guitar playing too. I don't want him letting me down. I'm going into the garden to practise a few stunt jumps right now . . .

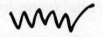

Well, that was a bad idea. When I got into the garden I made a ramp out of a bit of the fence that had fallen down and decided to start small by jumping over the flowerbeds. BIG MISTAKE. Turns out I need just a bit more practice.

When Mum saw that I'd skidded all over her flowers she locked my bike in the shed. PERFECT. How am I supposed to become a stuntboy if I don't even have a bike?

My life can't get any worse. Everyone at school thinks I'm a loser, Mum and Dad have grounded me, I'll never win the talent show and I'll probably never taste another bowl of Coco Snaps in my life! STUPID DIARY! Why did I ever start writing it in the first place? Look what trouble it's got me into! I told you I wasn't a diary person. Why didn't I listen? I could write anything and it wouldn't matter. Watch, here goes:

I wish my dad would turn bright green, my mum's hair would fall out and my sister would become a poodle. Oh, and GIVE ME BACK MY BIKE!

Like that's going to happen . . .

SATURDAY

What did I tell you?

This diary is NOT magic

Nothing has changed. Mum still has her hair, Dad is still his usual shade of pink, and my sister is not a poodle. Most importantly, my bike is still very much locked in the shed. I knew nothing would change, but a teeny weeny bit of me hoped that it might.

This diary has got me into so much trouble. When I realised everything was still the same I thought about throwing it straight in the bin. But then I remembered the future millions it's going to make me so I've decided to keep writing in it until after the talent show at least.

When I went downstairs this morning Mum and Dad were still cross with me and **ELLIE** was still grinning like a clown at a custard pie chucking contest.

To make matters worse **ELLIE** was being extra polite to Mum and Dad, which only made me look extra naughty by comparison. And that was unfair because I hadn't even done anything wrong today. It was only nine o'clock!

Once we'd all had breakfast **ELLIE** offered to unload the dishwasher. Mum shook her head and said that as I was the one who'd been naughty I should do it. That was just perfect. And all morning, every time **ELLIE** offered to be helpful, Mum ended up giving me another job to do — and **ELLIE** knew it so she made the most of it!

I wanted to go back upstairs, cover my head with the duvet and pretend today wasn't happening. <u>But no such luck.</u> I'd forgotten that it was Gran's birthday and we were all going to her house for a party. I had to get changed into 'something appropriate'. Which we all know is mum-speak for 'something hideously embarrassing'. By the time she'd finished,

I ended up looking like a butler.

ELLIE came downstairs dressed as Princess Jasmine from a cartoon she'd just watched. And Mum said **NOTHING**! I wasn't sure how that counted as 'something appropriate' but apparently it did.

On the way to Gran's house **ELLIE** asked Dad if she could choose the music because she'd been such a good girl. She was really rubbing it in. We drove for an hour and a half listening to the new ChaRLiE DiMPLES album. Her favourite, 'MY SQUiSHY WiSHY', is just

<u>the worst.</u> I ended up knowing all the words even though I really didn't want to.

By the time we got to Gran's house my ears had melted. I mean, what is a squishy wishy anyway?

WHAT IS A SQUISHY WISHY?

A)   A NEW SWEET
B)   A DEAD HEDGEHOG
C)   A PARTICULARLY JUICY FACE PIMPLE

TRICK QUESTION! IT'S ALL THREE!!

Gran had invited loads of her friends to her party so the garden was full of old people dancing badly to rubbish music. These people knew how to party — NOT! I was about to liven things up and put on **X-WING** when Gran stopped me and put on 'Stairway to

Heaven' instead, that song that Mr Burchester was so keen on, which seemed a little bit inconsiderate at a party full of old people, quite frankly. Apparently it didn't matter what I thought because I wasn't here to enjoy myself, Mum said. In fact, she told me that as I was grounded, I was lucky to be allowed to come to the party, and I could at least 'help out'. Which we all know is mum-speak for 'be her personal slave'.

Mum handed me a plate of tuna sandwiches and told me to offer it round. I spent the next half an hour trying to force-feed old people sandwiches while being stalked by Gran's terrifying cat, Mr Yummy Whiskers.

Don't ask! Gran let **ELLIE** name him. In the end I lured Mr Yummy Whiskers behind the shed and gave him the lot.

But if you thought that was the end of my list of jobs you'd be wrong. Mum took me into the kitchen and told me to do the washing-up. It was not fair — **ELLIE** was doing NOTHING. Worse than nothing, actually — she was showing all the old people her Princess Jasmine dance.

For some reason they loved it! HONESTLY!

The washing-up took ages and by the time I'd finished, my hands looked like a pair of prunes. I headed outside just in time for party games. Who knew that old people still played party games? And not party games for old people, like Whose Teeth are These?, Pass the Walking Stick, or Shave My Chin Whiskers either. No, real party games like Pass the Parcel and Charades. Charades took forever. There was a film called Gone With the Wind, which nobody could get. I'd have just made a farting noise and waved.

After the birthday cake, which had so many candles on top it looked like it was on fire, it was time for Gran's presents. Mum and Dad always bought the present and card and just put mine and **ELLIE**'s names on it. But after they had handed over the gift from all of us, **ELLIE** announced that she'd got an extra special surprise. She had made one of the most horrible things I've ever seen — <u>a birthday card for Gran!</u>

It turned out she had also made up a poem and written it inside the card. Everyone stood and smiled as she read it out loud.

Gran is nice,
Gran is sweet,
Gran is lovely,
Gran is kind,
Gran is pretty,
Gran is smiley-wiley!

It didn't even rhyme! And smiley-wiley isn't a word! I blamed Charlie Dimples for that.

If he could have a hit with 'MY SQUISHY WISHY' was it any wonder that six-year-old girls were making up words left, right and centre? But apparently that didn't matter. It was the thought that counted and the old people loved it. **ELLIE** is such a suck-up!

Just then Mr Yummy Whiskers staggered out from behind the shed and threw up a whole trayful of tuna sandwiches right in front of everybody. Luckily, I don't think anyone realised it was my fault. Unluckily, I had to clear it up anyway.

While we were in the car on the way home, listening to another hour and a half of CHARLIE DIMPLES, **ELLIE** waved a five-pound note in front of me. 'Gran gave it to me to say thank you for such a thoughtful birthday card,' she told me.

THAT IS SO UNFAIR! I should be the one getting paid. I was the one who did ALL the work at the party!

I was still none the wiser as to what a squishy wishy was when we got home, and I was really fed up. Before this day could get any worse I decided to come up here to my bedroom.

I really wish I'd remembered Gran's birthday and written her a poem this morning. Then she'd have given me five pounds, too. At least my poem would have rhymed! It can't be that hard to write something that she'd have been impressed by.

107

Something like,

Grandma, you smell
of lavender and rose,
I love your hair,
I love your toes,
You bring me such
supreme delight,
Every time you kiss me
goodnight.

There! That's worth five pounds of anybody's money. Too late now, though, isn't it? Maybe next year. **ELLIE**'s rich and I'm in Gran's bad books. I hate my life.

SUNDAY

When I woke up this morning there was a five-pound note lying on my pillow next to a letter. Now either the tooth fairy is being incredibly generous, or my ear has turned into a cash machine . . . or this diary has been up to its old tricks again!

I picked up the letter and had a look. Sure enough it was from Gran. She was thanking me for the wonderful poem I'd written for her birthday!

Now don't get me wrong, I was happy to have five pounds. It'll come in very useful . . .

But you and I both know I <u>didn't</u> write a poem. Well I did, but I wrote it down here, in this diary after the party . . .

Now I'm just confused! Sometimes the diary changes things and sometimes it doesn't! IS IT MAGIC OR ISN'T IT? I wish it would make its mind up. It's like an old man at a cake counter.

Anyway, I decided to go downstairs and see what else the diary had changed.

But **ELLIE** was still grinning and my bike was still locked in the shed so nothing was different there.

I thought I'd better try to get back into Mum and Dad's good books the old-fashioned way — by sucking up. That meant I had one of the worst Sundays of my life (and I once spent a whole Sunday de-gunking Uncle Rory's sink, so I know what I'm talking about).

I started by doing the washing-up and drying-up, then I washed Dad's car — WITHOUT BEING ASKED. To be honest, that's the best bad job there is. You get to use the hose and if next door's dog happens to walk past (which it always does) then it turns into target practice. After that I mowed the lawn, raked up leaves and even set the table for dinner — all of this without being asked! I've never worked so hard in all my life. Being good is exhausting. No wonder being bad's all the rage.

By the time we'd finished dinner I was so tired I couldn't even be bothered to argue with **ELLIE** over what we watched on TV. And believe me, that's a big deal because PRINCESS TWINKLE'S MAGIC CASTLE isn't bad — it's ABSOLUTELY AWFUL! And it has the most annoying theme tune ever:

PRINCESS TWINKLE IS NICE AND KIND,
SHE'S THE TWINKLIEST PRINCESS
YOU'LL EVER FIND,
SHE LIVES IN A WORLD
OF SPARKLES AND FLOWERS
IN A CASTLE MADE OF
CANDYFLOSS TOWERS!

It gets stuck in your head and by the time we'd finished watching SIX episodes I decided it was time for bed. Just as I was heading for the stairs, Mum stopped me. She'd noticed how much I'd been trying to make up for my behaviour and said I could have my bike back tomorrow. Result!

I was so happy that as I climbed the stairs I started to sing, but I realised I wasn't singing anything cool, like *X-WING* — I was singing the PRINCESS TWINKLE theme tune! As if it wasn't bad enough that I knew all the words to 'MY SQUISHY WISHY'! See what being good does to your brain? I decided to change the words to the PRINCESS TWINKLE song to make it better . . .

PRINCESS TWINKLE
is annoying and dumb,
I want to kick her up the bum.
She lives in a world of annoying
talking flowers
And her bloomin' show
goes on for hours!

What am I thinking? Nothing could make PRINCESS TWINKLE better.

While I was getting ready for bed I spotted the five-pound note on my dressing table next to this diary. Something's going on here, but I don't know what. I decided to write this entry to try and figure out when the diary changes things.

THINGS CHANGED WHEN:

* I knew what I wanted to say to **BRAD** and **CLAUDIA**
* I wished I'd revised for my maths test
* I wanted to have written a poem for Gran.

But it DIDN'T change anything when:

* I wanted other people to forget I was naughty at school
* I wanted to turn my sister into a poodle or turn my dad green.

I've spent ages thinking about it, and I MAY have figured it out. I THINK I can only change the things I've said and done (or not said and done). I can't change what other people have said and done, or what they think.

I suppose that makes sense. This is my diary so it can only change the things I do and say.

If this is right, then last time I wished for the wrong things — my wishes were all about other people. Instead I need to write about ME. So here goes . . .

→ I, **FIN SPENCER**, should never have tried to write on the walls.

→ I, **FIN SPENCER**, should never have misbehaved in lessons.

→ I, **FIN SPENCER**, should never have started a food fight.

→ I, **FIN SPENCER**, should never have worn an **X-WING** T-shirt and trainers to school.

→ I, **FIN SPENCER**, should never have been mean to **JOSH** at school, even though sometimes he deserves it!

In fact, on Friday I, **FIN SPENCER**, should have been the best-behaved boy any teacher had ever seen.

RIGHT! That's it. I'm off to bed. Let's see if this diary works its magic tonight. I can't really believe I'm trusting a diary to sort out my life. I'll have to think about punching myself in the face if this still doesn't work.

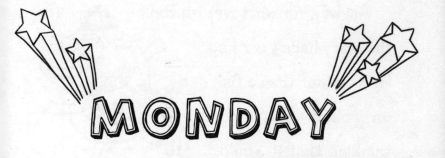

MONDAY

Okay, remember what I wrote yesterday about punching myself in the face? I didn't mean it. Because when I got into the kitchen this morning Mum and Dad still remembered what had happened at school last week. To be honest, that was better than it could have been. At least I wasn't in any more trouble. I could have come downstairs to find out I was being blamed for something else entirely. That has happened before. Sometimes I think I cause trouble in my sleep.

Anyway, for whatever reason, the diary hadn't worked. I'm stupider than a fish on roller-skates for thinking that it would.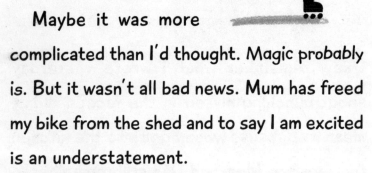

Maybe it was more complicated than I'd thought. Magic probably is. But it wasn't all bad news. Mum has freed my bike from the shed and to say I am excited is an understatement.

It was just in the nick of time too, because I remembered **JOSH** and I were supposed to be practising our big stunt in the playground after school. Hopefully some of my fincredibleness will rub off on him.

As Mum was handing my bike over she arched an eyebrow and said that this didn't mean everything was forgotten, but if I kept behaving like I had this weekend then I might get to go to the concert on Saturday.

Double result! ***X-WING*** is back on and Mum and Dad have definitely got tickets. I was so pleased I could have kissed them both. I could have, but I didn't.

That had put me in such a good mood that I even took an interest in the 'Kids Say the Sweetest Things' cartoon that Dad was reading. There was a picture of a reeeeeally long sausage dog walking down the street and that snot-nosed kid was back.

This time he was pointing at the dog and saying, 'Wowzer, Daddy! That dog must have eaten a lot of sausages to look like that!'

I even pretended to find it funny and laughed out loud. Maybe I overdid it a bit. Dad looked at me like I'd gone mad and said, 'It's not that funny!'

OH, COME ON! I know it's not that funny. It's never that funny. I've been trying to tell both my parents that for the past five years but that hasn't stopped them laughing like hyenas every morning, has it? What do you have to do to please these people? I just don't get grown-ups.

The **X-WING** advert was still there, only it was now covered with a huge **SOLD OUT** banner.

Luckily Mum and Dad have already got tickets so as long as I don't do anything stupid I'll be there!

At school, after I'd chained up my bike in the bike sheds, I went into class and checked with **JOSH** that we were still on for stunt practice later. He gave me a double thumbs-up and pointed to the guitar case propped up against the chair. Then he said that over the weekend his mum had had a great idea — his sister, **MEGAN**, plays the tuba and he thought it would be great if she could be involved in the talent-show stunt-jumping too.

I COULDN'T BELIEVE MY EARS. There is nothing stuntboy OR rock star about a tuba-trumping girl. Seriously, no matter how well you play the tuba it sounds like you're doing a fart. Sometimes **JOSH** gets it sooo wrong! No, scratch that. **JOSH** ALWAYS gets it sooo wrong. He's just lucky I'm always here to help him out.

I told him there was <u>no way</u> **MEGAN** and her tuba were being in my talent show-act. He muttered that it wasn't MY talent-show act, it was OUR talent-show act. That may be true, but it was my idea. I made him promise to tell **MEGAN** she wasn't needed and then the bell rang for lessons.

I could definitely do with a *better best* mate.

Apart from that, school was fine. It seemed like all the apologies I'd made last week had paid off. In class, Mrs Johnson gave me the old 'new week, new start' speech that she usually reserves for **BRAD RADLEY**, and I promised to work hard and not get into trouble. She nodded and said, 'We'll hear no more about it,' which we all know is teacher-speak for 'Cross me again and I'll drag this up to haunt you in an instant!' As I was taking my seat she said,

'It's nice to have the old FIN back. You're normally such a sweet boy.'

The whole class started to laugh and I was so embarrassed that my face went redder than a baboon's bum.

After school **JOSH** met me by the bike rack to practise our stunt. **MEGAN** turned up too. Because **JOSH** is technically my assistant I made him drag a couple of bricks and some planks of wood out into the middle of the playground so I could get my jumping right.

I had a go at persuading **JOSH**'s sister to lie down so I could jump over her, but she refused. When I told her she couldn't play her farty tuba, she just sat next to her massive tuba case and sulked. **JOSH** unpacked his guitar and slung it over his shoulder. I was psyching myself up when **JOSH** started to tune the thing. I gave him a look and he stopped. This stunt needed total concentration. I was just starting my run up when **JOSH** began playing his guitar. It sounded like someone strangling an octopus.

I did my best to block it out, but then **JOSH** started doing all of these weird rock-star poses, jumping in the air, falling to his knees, something he called 'the windmill' . . .

I was so distracted that I missed the jump entirely and crashed into a tree. **JOSH** asked if that was supposed to happen. NO, IT WAS NOT! He was supposed to be my backing guitarist. Backing guitarists did not do 'the windmill'. Backing guitarists stood in one place and let the star of the show get on with it.

We were just about to have another go when **JOSH** asked about the talent-show prize and who was going to keep it. It turns out that he's broken his phone and would quite like a new one. I told him that as I was doing the dangerous bit of the stunt I should keep it. He could have the trophy. **JOSH** wasn't happy. He thought that his part was quite dangerous too — apparently I'd nearly run him over. I tried to explain that I wouldn't have nearly run him over if he'd stayed in one place like a normal person, but he wasn't listening. He thought we should split the prize. HOW DO YOU SPLIT A PHONE?

JOSH can be so stupid sometimes. I told him that we'd think of something (which he doesn't seem to know is Fin-speak for 'I'll keep it!') and had another go at the jump.

I was about to ride over the planks when this massive

PAAAAARP!

came out of nowhere. I was so startled I crashed into the tree again. As I was picking myself up I saw **JOSH**'s sister laughing at me. She was holding her tuba. It turns out **MEGAN** is just as annoying as **JOSH**. I called our practice to a halt and headed home.

JOSH was lucky I was even letting him be in my talent-show act and now he wants to keep the prize too! I was the one risking life and limb! I should have told **JOSH** that I didn't want him in my act, and have been done with it. I should have told him that he's nothing but the guitar-playing assistant. **ANYBODY** could do that job, and if he thinks he's going to get his fingers on that phone then he's got another think coming! **JOSH** needs to pay more attention and do things my way. I'm the star here!

Let's hope I can knock him into shape tomorrow, before I knock myself into another tree.

TUESDAY

So today did not go exactly to plan. When I got to school this morning I saw **JOSH** by the lockers, obviously trying to avoid me. From the look on his face I could tell that he was upset. It's harder to upset **JOSH** than you might think, by the way, as **JOSH** doesn't really show his emotions. When you've been best buddies for as long as we have, though, you get to notice little things. His nostrils were twitching like a bunny in a carrot factory. That meant he was upset.

I soon found out why. It seemed like this diary had decided to work again! Everything I wrote down last night about what I should have told **JOSH** was exactly what he thought I had told him. So he remembers me telling him that I was the star, that he should do as I say and that I was keeping the phone when we won. Which is all true, of course. I suppose the diary just saved me the effort of having to tell him to his face — which I would never have done . . .

Apparently, **JOSH** thinks that I've turned into a real bossy boots and I'm far too demanding. Well, excuse me for wanting to get something right for once! **JOSH** has decided to enter the talent show on his own and win the phone by himself . . . and we're not best friends any more. Which, quite frankly, is a relief. He's been dragging me down for far too long. And as for winning the talent show? **DON'T MAKE ME LAUGH!** What's he going to do – a Dweeb Dance? He doesn't stand a chance against a stuntboy like me!

As I went into registration **BRAD RADLEY** appeared. He'd seen everything that had just happened and thought **JOSH** was throwing away the opportunity of a lifetime. **BRAD** knew my talent-show stunt was going to be so fincredible there was no point in anyone else even entering. **BRAD RADLEY** was right. Then it struck me – **BRAD RADLEY** usually is right, it's just that in the past I was being too much of a loser to listen. Kids like me could learn a lot from kids like **BRAD**. They show us our faults so we can do better next time. **BRAD** doesn't deserve a detention, he deserves a medal. Besides, since I gave him that talking to, he's been much nicer. At least some people can take criticism, unlike others I could mention — **JOSH DOYLE**.

BRAD offered to take **JOSH**'s place in my talent-show stunt. He said it would be an honour and a privilege to be a part of something so fincredible and he promised he would stand at the side and play the guitar. What's more, he said I could keep the phone for myself when we won because he'd already got one. **THINGS CAN'T GET ANY BETTER.**

With **BRAD** on my side I can't lose! We agreed to practise after school.

All through lessons **JOSH** gave me the cold shoulder. So childish. I gave him the cold shoulder right back.

After lunch we had art class. We'd been making vases out of clay for the past six weeks. We'd designed them, moulded them and then put them in the kiln. Today it was finally time to decorate them. **CLAUDIA RONSON**'s vase was amazing. Mine was less good, but at least it was better than **JOSH**'s, which looked like a poo from a very ill dog.

CLAUDIA'S VASE

FIN'S VASE

JOSH'S VASE

Anyway, art is one of those really cool classes where the teacher, Mrs Skiffington, lets you talk while you're working. My workbench was right in front of **CLAUDIA**'s and everybody was busy decorating their vases (or dog poos if your name is **JOSH DOYLE**). **BRAD** and I started talking about how great the talent show was going to be. **BRAD** asked me what **JOSH** was going to do now that he wasn't in my act. I laughed and said he'd probably do a Dweeb Dance. **BRAD** didn't know what a Dweeb Dance was. Nor did I really but I decided to show him anyway! I started to wiggle my bum and wave my arms about like a street-dancing scarecrow.

I was really getting into it and took a step back to make more room when I accidentally bumped into **CLAUDIA**'s workbench. Her vase started to wobble. Everything seemed to go into slow motion, like in one of those late-night horror movies I'm not supposed to watch.

At first I thought it was going to be all right. But it wasn't. **CLAUDIA**'s vase toppled off the bench. I jumped to catch it but missed and knocked the workbench again. This sent all of **CLAUDIA**'s friends' vases flying too.

Before I knew it, the floor was covered in broken pottery and **CLAUDIA** was staring at me like I'd just kicked a puppy. I tried to make things better by saying she could have my vase instead, but for some reason she didn't want it.

Mrs Skiffington gave me a dustpan and brush and made me clear up the mess.

As I was putting **CLAUDIA**'s and her friends' broken vases in the bin, Mrs Skiffington announced that from now on there would be no talking in class so that we could concentrate and avoid any more accidents. GREAT. Now everybody else in the class was angry with me too.

One thing is for certain, **CLAUDIA** definitely doesn't think I'm **FINCREDIBLE FIN** now.

At least things got better after school. **BRAD** is soooo much better than **JOSH** at playing the guitar. I didn't crash into a tree once and **BRAD** stood exactly where I told him, playing exciting bits during the run-up and shouting '**FIN THE FINCREDIBLE**' whenever I did something cool — which was

ALL THE TIME! He even filmed it on his phone so we could see where I was going wrong — which was NOWHERE!

By the time practice was over I was clearing the jump every time. This is going to be brilliant. I don't know why **BRAD** and I weren't friends ages ago! He's coming over to my house tomorrow night to practise some more.

The only bad thing about the day was smashing the vases. I wish I hadn't broken them. If I knew for certain how this diary worked then I might be able to fix them, but I don't. Sometimes it works and sometimes it doesn't. I know it only changes things I've said or done, but then when I said I wished I hadn't done all those things last week, nothing changed . . . I'm going to have another read back through what I've written and see if I can figure it out. My future marriage to **CLAUDIA RONSON** depends on it.

Well, maybe not. But it'd be nice to be able to ask her to the school disco or something.

It's now two hours later and I think I may have worked out the diary! Every time it has changed things it's been when I've written what I wished I'd said or done **ON THE DAY** that I've done it! It doesn't seem to work when I've left it for a while. So it didn't work with all the school stuff because I tried to fix it three days later.

If I'm right, these are

FIN SPENCER'S
FINCREDIBLE
DIARY RULES

1. The diary only changes the things I say and do or wished I'd said and done

2. It only changes things if I write about what I wish I'd done ON THE DAY they happen

3. Diaries are still for losers. It's only this one that's cool.

So if I'm right, I can still try to change what happened with the vases today. Here goes.

Diary, I shouldn't have demonstrated the Dweeb Dance in art class. If I hadn't done that then I wouldn't have knocked over **CLAUDIA**'s vase and she might still be talking to me. Well, not talking to me exactly, but at least she wouldn't think I was a vase murderer.

Come on, diary. **I'M COUNTING ON YOU.**

WEDNESDAY

This morning I was so excited to see if the Fincredible Diary Rules were right that I skipped breakfast and went to school early. I was so early I even managed to arrive before the nerds. To be honest I didn't really fancy breakfast anyway. It's hard to get excited about a cereal that tastes of hedges.

Besides, I had to find out if **CLAUDIA**'s vase was miraculously back in one piece or not. If it wasn't she'd always think of me as a pesky pottery pulveriser — and try saying that three times fast!

When I got into the art room — guess what?!! The vase was back on the shelf looking better than ever, and so were all her friends' vases. The diary had worked its magic again! I took **CLAUDIA**'s vase down to check for cracks — it was perfect! I gave it a little kiss before I put it back on the shelf.

It was only then that I noticed Mrs Skiffington watching me through her office window. Brilliant. Now she thinks I snog pottery in my spare time.

Never mind. The vases were fine and that was all that mattered! Not that **CLAUDIA** noticed or anything. BUT WHY WOULD SHE?

As far as she was concerned there was nothing to fix in the first place. The wedding is back on. Or at least it will be when **CLAUDIA** realises I exist. AGAIN.

For the first time in ages school felt normal, which was a relief. Whenever I saw **JOSH** he was sulking, the big baby, but luckily I now have **BRAD** to hang around with.

When I got home things looked bad — **ELLIE** was smiling at me. As we all know, this usually means only one thing, and I started to worry about what I'd done wrong. I couldn't think of anything but that means nothing.

I needn't have worried. For once, **ELLIE** wasn't smiling because I was in trouble, she was smiling because her best friends, Chloe and Porsche, had come for a sleepover.

A SLEEPOVER IN THE MIDDLE OF THE WEEK?

It turns out their school's closed tomorrow for teacher training! Not that you can call the place they go to a proper school — it's all skipping and colouring-in as far as I can tell. And who calls their daughter Porsche, anyway? I bet her dad calls their car Rebecca or something.

I was about to go to my room to play on my Xbox when Mum stopped me. Dad had been 'held up at work' and she needed to pop to the shops for more ketchup, so she wanted me to look after the girls for a minute or two. I couldn't believe Mum fell for that one! Everyone knows that 'held up at work' is dad-speak for 'hanging out with my mates until the coast is clear.'

I was going to make up some excuse but Mum guessed that's what I was going to do before I could say anything.

'I hope you're not going to make some excuse and then go up to your room to play on your Xbox,' she said. 'Because I need you to properly keep an eye on them while I'm gone. I won't be long and I'm trusting you to look out for them.'

I was about to ignore her and go to play on my Xbox anyway when she read my mind AGAIN. She said that I could play on my Xbox if I wanted — and I did want — but if I also wanted to go to the concert on Saturday — and I did also want to — then I should help her out with the little-sister-and-her-friends-sitting.

I couldn't believe it! I WAS BEING BLACKMAILED BY MY OWN MOTHER!

I had no choice, so I went to see what the three little piggies were doing. It was worse than I'd imagined. Before I even got to **ELLIE**'s bedroom door I could hear them. They were singing 'MY SQUISHY WISHY' into hairbrush microphones at the top of their voices. Seriously, you could hear them on the moon.

When **ELLIE** saw me she wanted me to join in and handed me a hairbrush. No way! Helping Mum with the girls did NOT include singing Charlie Dimples' songs into a hairbrush. I was about to tell **ELLIE** that when Mum appeared at the door to say goodbye and

said how nice it was that I was 'joining in'.
Which we all know is mum-speak for
'Take the hairbrush or I'll tear those
X-WING tickets to pieces!' I knew what
I had to do . . .

IT WAS THE WORST MOMENT OF MY LIFE SO
FAR. SERIOUSLY. THE. WORST. MOMENT.

X-WING had better be worth it.

The song finished and I threw the
microphone — I mean hairbrush — onto **ELLIE**'s
bed. **ELLIE** smiled at me and told me to sing
it again. NO WAY! Once was enough! I might
actually start to like the song or something.
But then I realised that if I didn't do what
ELLIE asked, she'd tell Mum that I hadn't
been joining in and we all know what that

means. No **X-WING** concert. I was trapped!
I picked up the hairbrush and sang for all
I was worth.

Sometimes I hate my sister. NO! Scratch
that. I ALWAYS hate my sister.

As I was getting to the end of
'MY SQUISHY WISHY' for the second time,
ELLIE turned off the music and announced
that it was time for a dolly's picnic in the
garden. So that I didn't feel left out **ELLIE**
handed me her spare dolly — Penelope
Fuzzyface — and, holding my hand, she led
me to the garden with her friends.

Penelope Fuzzyface is TERRIFYING. When
ELLIE was little she used to suck Penelope's
nose and now she looks like a hundred horror

movie baddies all rolled into one!

It wasn't all bad, though. Mum had left some cakes and stuff for the picnic and I got to eat as much cake as I wanted. Normally Mum made me stop after one slice, but it seems that when it's a picnic for dollies you can eat as much as you like and then blame it on the dolly. Clever, huh?

As I was polishing off my eighth jam tart **ELLIE** and the girls decided that it would be fun if they gave me a makeover. I spat jammy crumbs all over Penelope Fuzzyface — which was actually an improvement — and shook my head. I would do a lot of things for my sister . . . No, hang on, I would do NOTHING for my sister, but on the other hand I would do a lot of things for *X-WING* tickets. So I closed my eyes, thought of *X-WING*, and kissed goodbye to my beautiful face. (Which is hard to do.)

When they'd finished, Ferrari, or whatever her name, is handed me a mirror. I looked like I'd been caught inside an exploding make-up shop.

ELLIE thought I looked just like ChaRLie DiMPLeS. Which was kind of true, if Charlie Dimples looked like he'd been caught inside an exploding make-up shop.

She gave me the hairbrush they'd been using to style my hair and asked me to sing 'MY SQUISHY WISHY' again. By now I had no pride, so I pretended to be really enthusiastic. I was getting to the chorus when

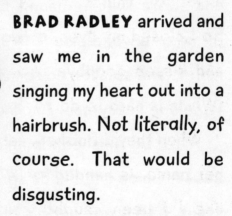

BRAD RADLEY arrived and saw me in the garden singing my heart out into a hairbrush. Not literally, of course. That would be disgusting.

Either way, it was a disaster!

WORST. MOMENT. EVER.

I'd forgotten he was coming over to practise the talent-show stunt. He stared at me for what felt like forever and then I saw that he was holding his phone. A shiver ran down my spine. He hadn't taken a photo, had he?

I rushed over and demanded to see his phone, but **BRAD** put it back in his pocket and swore that he hadn't taken any photos of me or anyone else. I breathed a sigh of relief (and splattered runny lipstick all over Penelope Fuzzyface. <u>Another improvement</u>).

After I'd finished wiping off the make-up, **ELLIE**, Chloe and Skoda agreed to watch our stunt. **BRAD** got out his guitar and started to strum while I got the ramp ready. I wasn't going to jump over anything today — I just wanted to practise my take-offs and landings.

BRAD played as I cycled towards the ramp. Ellie, Chloe and Nissan watched and the stunt went perfectly! Even the dollies looked impressed. (Apart from Penelope Fuzzyface who looked terrifying, as usual.)

Then **BRAD** had a brainwave. Why didn't we practise the stunt again but this time jump over the dollies? I thought it was a great idea but Porsche wasn't so sure. She didn't want her dolly to get dirty. But who listens to a girl who's named after a car? We took the dollies and lined them up in front of the ramp.

The run up was perfect. **BRAD** was singing and wiggling his leg like a rock star. But when

I hit the ramp there was a loud

SNAP!

The ramp had broken and I ended up cycling right over the dollies' heads. Porsche started to cry, which made her sound more like a car than ever! Maybe that's why her parents called her Porsche in the first place.

ELLIE was shouting at me that Penelope Fuzzyface was ruined forever, although I thought it was definitely an improvement.

Then **ELLIE** started to cry too and Chloe was definitely thinking about it. Mum arrived back just at that moment. When she saw the crying girls and the dolly carnage she

dropped the ketchup bottle on the floor. She was not happy. **BRAD** was sent home and suddenly I was being accused of dolly murder.

Chloe and Porsche wanted to go home too, so Mum had to drive them. As she slammed the car door, sleepover ruined, she sent me to my room. The concert was off again.

It's so unfair. Why do parents always remember the one thing you did wrong instead of all the amazing things you did right? It wasn't my fault the ramp broke. I should never have tried to jump over the dollies in the first place. Everything was fine up until then. If I hadn't tried to jump over the dollies then I'd still be going to see **X-WING** on Saturday, wouldn't I? Luckily I know a way to fix it . . .

Diary, I shouldn't have tried to jump over the dollies on my bicycle. IF YOU CAN CHANGE THAT I'LL LOVE YOU FOREVER.

THURSDAY

When I went into the kitchen this morning, Mum, Dad and **ELLIE** were smiling at me. Chloe and Porsche were there and they were smiling too. At first I was worried. Everybody smiling at me like that must mean I'd done something mega bad, right? But no! They were smiling because they were pleased with me! Apparently that can happen too — who knew? Yesterday **FIN SPENCER** was apparently a model son and brother and best-friends-of-little-sister entertainer.

The only person around that table not smiling was Penelope Fuzzyface. But then she never smiles. I realised that the fact that Chloe and Porsche were still there meant they didn't go home last night and the sleepover had happened. **THANK YOU, DIARY!**

Mum thought my change of behaviour was down to the Keep Fit breakfast cereal she's been making me eat. Parents really know nothing, do they? My good behaviour was down to two very simple things — bribery and a magic diary!

As I was leaving for school I couldn't resist asking Dad how his mates were last night. Without thinking he just said, 'Fine, thanks!'

BUSTED! He wasn't 'held up at work' at all. Bet Dad wished he had a magic diary too when he saw Mum's face! She asked everyone but Dad to 'Leave the room for a minute'. Which was mum-speak for 'Stand back, Dad's gonna die'!

I felt a bit bad for him, but then I remembered that he hadn't had to sing into a hairbrush three times and be covered in make-up — he deserved everything that was coming to him.

I arrived at school with a smile on my face. Tomorrow **BRAD** and I would win the talent show and I'd have a phone and on Saturday I would go to see **X-WING**. All I had to do was keep a low profile until then and the perfect weekend would be coming my way.

But as I walked down the corridor people started to laugh at me. I checked I hadn't accidentally tucked my trousers into my socks — that's happened before. But not this time. It had to be something else. I saw **BRAD RADLEY** by my locker — maybe he knew why people were laughing.

BRAD smiled at me. It wasn't a nice smile, it was the smile a shark gives you just before it bites your legs off.

It turned out **BRAD** knew exactly why everybody was laughing at me. He pushed a button on his phone and a video began to play on the screen. When I realised what I was seeing I wanted to crawl into my locker and shut the door forever.

It was a video of me, in full CHARLIE

166

DiMPLES make-up, singing 'MY SQUiSHY WiSHY' at the top of my voice. What was BRAD playing at? I thought we were friends! He'd sworn that he hadn't taken any photos.

When I asked him about it he said, 'I didn't take any photos, but nobody said anything about videos.'

I needed to get his phone and smash it to pieces. I tried to grab it but BRAD held it high above my head so I couldn't reach. As I was standing there, hopping up and down like an ant in a tap-dancing contest, JOSH came over, waving his phone at me. He'd got the video too.

You look RIDICULOUS,

he said.

167

Now I really wanted to live in my locker forever. I didn't understand. How had **JOSH** got the video? **BRAD** grinned as he told me that EVERYONE in my class had the video. If you pushed the buttons on his phone in the right way you could send videos to everyone in the contacts list. And that was just what **BRAD** had done.

Why did **BRAD** do it? I thought we were fincredible best mates.

BRAD shook his head at me, when I asked him. He told me he'd never be best mates with a loser like me. Apparently he'd only ever pretended to be my friend so that he'd be close by when I did something embarrassing. Then he'd used it to get his own back for making him look stupid last week. He said he knew it would only be a matter of time, but he'd never imagined I'd do anything quite so ridiculous! Everyone had seen me singing and dancing to 'MY SQUISHY WISHY', or if they hadn't yet they soon would. I should never have trusted **BRAD RADLEY**.

WHAT WAS I THINKING?

School couldn't end soon enough. I spent break time and lunchtime hiding in the toilets. I thought I'd dodged everybody but I bumped into **CLAUDIA RONSON** on my way home. She gave me a smile and then turned to her friends and giggled.

PERFECT! She thinks I'm a loser too.

I know exactly what I have to do. I have

to leave my school forever and run away
to Pluto.

I'm back at home now and I've locked
myself in my room to write in this diary.

I couldn't face Mum and Dad and **ELLIE** after the day I've had. I guess I just have to hope that people will forget about the video when they see my cool stunt at the talent show tomorrow. . .

But as I've been writing I've realised something else. Brad won't be in my stunt now — not that I'd want him there anyway. I could ask Josh back, but I know exactly what he'd say.

Gotta go, I need to come up with a way of saving my talent-show act.

I'm back and feeling much better about things because I've realised something — I don't need any help. My stunt is going to be amazing without **BRAD** or **JOSH**. Sure, I might not have a live musical accompaniment, but the stunt-jumping should be enough to win the phone. I could play *X-WING* as a backing track. So I went to find ~~ELLIE~~ to see if she'd watch me practise jumping for a bit, but she was in the middle of a PRINCESS TWINKLE marathon and wouldn't budge.

I watched a bit of PRINCESS TWINKLE until I realised what I was doing and decided to go and do something more interesting instead — like rearrange my pencil-shavings collection.

When I was getting ready for bed I thought about how I could use this diary to change things. If I could fix it so that **BRAD** hadn't come round to my house yesterday then he wouldn't have got the video footage on his phone . . . But then I remembered the Fincredible Diary Rules. I can only change things that I do, not what **BRAD** did. And I can only change things on the day they happen — it's too late now. But that means I can do something to change what happened today. I should have stood up to **BRAD** a bit more today. It's much easier to write that here, in this diary — it's really hard when he's standing right in front of you. I should have told him that I was doing something nice for my sister and that there was nothing wrong with that. Quite frankly, he shouldn't take videos of people without asking anyway — if he's not careful he'll go through life with no friends at all.

So yes, diary, I wish I'd stood up more to **BRAD RADLEY** today.

I hope that works, but I'm beginning to realise that this diary has a nasty habit of backfiring on me.

FRIDAY

Today was talent-show day. The day I was to become a world famous stuntboy—rockstar! The day nothing was allowed to go wrong — right? WRONG! I knew it was going to be a bad day as soon as I'd had my first mouthful of Keep Fit breakfast cereal. Dad slammed the paper down on the table and gave me a really weird look. Did I have a volcano on my chin or something?

Before I could go and check, he pointed at me and then at the paper and started spluttering. At first I was scared. Had the video of me dancing in the garden gone viral? Had it made the headlines?

But no, he was pointing to 'Kids Say the Sweetest Things' cartoon. I had a closer look. The snot-nosed kid was back again, but this time in the cartoon he was reciting a poem. How sad. But then I realised he was reciting MY POEM! The poem I wrote for Grandma. Well, the poem I wrote in my diary for Grandma!

**Grandma, you smell
of lavender and rose,
I love your hair,**

I love your toes,
You bring me such
supreme delight,
Every time you kiss me
goodnight.

Gran loved the poem so much she had sent it into the paper and now they'd published it ALONG WITH MY NAME! Mum was proud, **ELLIE** was jealous and Dad seemed to understand exactly how I was feeling . . .

I knew that when the kids at school saw it I was going to be a laughing stock for the second day running. I tried to look on the bright side — how many kids at school would actually see 'Kids Say the Sweetest Things' cartoon anyway?

Turns out all of them do when your ex-friend **BRAD RADLEY** cuts out the cartoon and sticks it to your locker. Apparently what I said to him yesterday about ending up with no friends made him hate me more than ever — thanks, diary! I tore the cartoon up and flushed it down the toilet but it was too late. Everywhere I went people kept telling me that they loved my hairy toes. That was NOT what I wrote. Five pounds was not worth this.

Luckily, people soon forgot about the cartoon because they were getting excited about the talent show. It couldn't come soon enough. I needed to win it and restore my reputation. I was so sure I was going to win the phone I spent lunchtime collecting phone numbers to add to my new phone's contacts list.

The talent show took place in the hall after school. Mum and Dad came to watch and brought ELLIE too, who'd dressed up in her Princess Jasmine outfit for the occasion. Everyone kept stopping to tell us how cute she looked. I couldn't believe it! I was about to risk life and limb and all anyone was interested in was my sister's dress.

I had brought the old fish tank into school so I went and filled it with water from the art room and wound up my shark to check it was still working. It was going to be amazing. Just before I went backstage, Dad ruffled my hair and said 'Do your best.' Which we all know is dad-speak for 'Win this thing or you're never coming home.'

Watching the first few acts I knew I had nothing to worry about. Peter Bishop spun four plates on sticks and smashed three of them, one of them on Mr Finch's toe. Olivia Sanderson did a ventriloquist act with a dummy, but the head kept popping off and making the little kids in the front row cry. (The dummy's head that is, not Olivia's head. If Olivia's head had popped off that would have been an act.) Then Paddy Horgan came on and armpit-farted the National Anthem. Luckily he got dragged off before he could be beheaded for treason!

The phone was in the bag. MY bag.

After the interval I took to the stage and positioned my ramps. I was using some of the sports equipment from the gym cupboard.

Then I got my bike, stood centre stage and told the audience what I was about to do.

'Ladies and gentlemen, boys and girls! Do not try this at home!' I shouted. 'I, **FINCREDIBLE FIN SPENCER** — aka Stuntboy — am going to jump over a shark tank!'

At this everyone gasped and then I revealed my fish tank and the wind-up shark and they all laughed. This was going perfectly! I had them in the palm of my hand. I nodded to Mr Finch who was manning the sound desk and ***X-WING*** started to blare through the school speakers. From the stage I saw Mr Burchester shove his fingers in his ears. Seriously! That man has no right to call himself a music teacher!

I tried not to let it annoy me and prepared for my run-up.

Now I'd never actually done the whole routine all the way through before, and the last time I practised jumping over anything I'd crushed a lot of dollies. But there was something about the crowd and the lights and the fact that everyone was looking at me that made me feel strangely confident. From the stage I looked out onto the audience and I saw Dad, Mum and **ELLIE** staring back at me. They were hard to miss. **ELLIE** was dressed as Princess Jasmine, after all!

As I set off towards the ramp everything seemed to go in slow motion. I saw **CLAUDIA RONSON** watching my every move. As I hit the jump, I lifted my weight, just like I'd been practising — and for once everything went according to plan!

I jumped over the shark tank and landed on the other side. IT WAS AMAZING!

As I left the stage I waved to my fans and looked forward to owning a brand new phone.

The next few acts were nothing to worry about, and then, to close the show, it was ~~super-dweeb JOSH DOYLE~~. As he'd only decided to enter a few days ago they'd tagged him onto the end. I couldn't wait to see what he was going to do — it was guaranteed to be awful!

He went to the centre of the stage and then waved to his sister, who was standing in the wings, to join him. I tried not to smirk as she came on stage carrying her tuba.

'**MEGAN** and I are going to do a duet!' he announced.

The crowd went 'Aaah!' Bunch of saps.

'It's a song we've written about the school!'

I could hardly believe what I was hearing. **JOSH** was actually going to stand in front of the whole school and sing a song about the school to a tuba accompaniment!

JOSH started to sing and his sister started parping.

My school is the best!
My school is the tops!
My school beats the rest!
My school rocks!

I started to laugh. But then I realised that I was the only one who was laughing, because **JOSH** has an amazing voice! As I looked around the audience I could see all the girls — even **CLAUDIA RONSON** — smiling and nodding along. Mrs Johnson was rocking her head in time to the beat and MY OWN MOTHER was wiping away a tear.

What is wrong with these people?

Then **JOSH**'s sister put down the tuba and started to beatbox! Who knew she could do that? And **JOSH** started to rap.

There's Burchester and Bucklestrap, Johnson and Finch too, But what really makes my school special is every one of you!

And then **JOSH** pointed to everyone in the hall — and they loved it. **MEGAN** picked up the tuba and **JOSH** sang the verse again, and by the time he'd finished, the whole audience was on their feet clapping like seals at a fish factory!

I was worried. **JOSH** had sung a song about everybody in the audience and told them they were the best. But I had risked life and limb to win this contest — surely I didn't need to panic? They weren't going to fall for a suck-up song about school, were they?

Turns out they were going to! Four of the judges were mentioned in the song, for goodness sake! Mr Finch stood on the stage to announce the winners — **JOSH** and **MEGAN DOYLE**. Josh had won my phone. Apparently **JOSH**'s song was 'original, simple and beautiful'. Which we all know is teacher-speak

for 'cringey, soppy and sucky'. Then Mr
Finch added that it was nice to see a brother
and sister working in harmony, which everyone
laughed at. I wanted to be sick.

JOSH took the phone and gave me a really
smug look as if to say, 'Told you so'.

Then he held it up for everyone to see.

SHOW-OFF!

All the way home Mum kept telling me not
to be a sore loser. Which was mum-speak for
'You should tell **JOSH DOYLE** how great
his act was.' I was not having it. I had worked
hard for that phone. It should be mine and
I knew exactly how to get it. I came straight
upstairs to write in this diary . . .

If the judges think a suck-up song about

188

school is better than a death-defying stunt then a suck-up song about school was what I should have done. I should have got my sister up on stage too. She could have danced around like she did at the birthday party. If they want cute, they can have cute!

Are you listening, diary?

I should never have done my stunt-jumping at the talent show today. I should have written a song about school just like **JOSH**'s. Better than **JOSH**'s. Something like:

**I love school and all the
teachers too,
No one loves school
as much as I do!**

I love art and maths
and music and French,
I love sitting in the classroom
or on the canteen bench.

The school food is delicious,
I'm sad when the day is through
Misters Finch, Burchester and
Bucklestrap — I love you!

SUCK-UP ENOUGH?

Then I should have got up very early this morning to practise and I should have practised every spare moment of today until I sounded better than Charlie Dimples himself — NOT HARD. And I should have woken ELLIE up early to practise the dance.

Then I should have won that phone.

Right. Now I'm going to bed and if I don't have a phone when I wake up there'll be trouble.

SATURDAY

THANK YOU, DIARY! THANK YOU, THANK YOU, THANK YOU! The perfect day has started perfectly. I've woken up to find a phone on my pillow. This can only mean one of three things.

1. MY EAR HAS TURNED INTO A MOBILE PHONE SHOP OVERNIGHT

2. THE TOOTH FAIRY HAS GOT EVEN MORE GENEROUS

3. THE DIARY HAS WORKED AND I WON THE SCHOOL TALENT SHOW!

I've taken the phone out of the packaging and plugged it in. I want it to be fully charged for the **X-WING** concert tonight. Now, for breakfast . . .

www

So, when I got downstairs this morning Mum had put the talent-show trophy on the breakfast table. I'd forgotten there even was a trophy. But there it was, and I must have won it because my name was on the bottom.

After breakfast I spent all morning typing numbers into my new phone and by eleven o'clock my thumbs hurt and I'd gone a bit cross-eyed. But it didn't matter because my contacts list was bulging and **FIN SPENCER** was finally connected to the twenty-first century.

To celebrate, I headed down to the shop for a can of lemonade. As I was going in I bumped into **JOSH** coming out. He was very angry. He said I must have somehow found out about his idea for the talent show and copied it. Which I sort of did, I suppose. This diary had fixed it that yesterday we BOTH sang a song about school. But because I went on first, and everyone knew **JOSH** was a late entry, they all thought it was

JOSH who had copied my idea rather than the other way round. **JOSH** reckoned I'd made him look stupid. I told him that he didn't need my help to do that.

JOSH said he was never going to speak to me again, which was ironic considering I finally had a phone he could call me on! But I couldn't help feeling a bit guilty.

The afternoon felt like it went on forever. Normally I'd play **DEATH SQUADRON** with **JOSH** on my Xbox but we all knew that wasn't going to happen. I decided to play with my little sister instead, but she just didn't get it.

After two hours of beating **ELLIE** again and again I gave up. I suppose I should have taught her how to play the game first, but where would be the fun in that?

Finally, it was time to get ready to go to the concert. I got out my favourite **X-WING** T-shirt and the sunnies I saved for special occasions. I looked at myself in the mirror but the glasses were too dark to see properly and I ended up falling into the wardrobe. Never mind — nothing was going to spoil this evening. I popped my new phone into my pocket and headed downstairs.

In the car Mum and Dad were really excited and so was **ELLIE**. Which was weird. I never knew she was a big **X-WING** fan. Maybe there was hope for her after all.

Dad turned on the radio and popped in the **CHARLIE DIMPLES** CD 'to get us in the mood'. I laughed — good one, Dad! He could be quite funny sometimes. I even found myself singing along when 'MY SQUISHY WISHY' came on. I'd been brainwashed! As we got close to the stadium the butterflies were back in my tummy.

But when we actually got to the stadium a strange thing happened — we drove right past it. Maybe Dad knew a good place to park. Dads are like that — they drive past a hundred perfect parking spaces just to park in one that, for some reason, they like best. Who knows what's going on in their heads?

Dad finally decided to park the car at the venue where CHARLIE DIMPLES was playing. I was confused. Was he trying to be funny again? Because if he was it was NOT WORKING! But when he turned off the engine and Mum got out of the car I realised nobody was joking about anything. We were at the CharLie DiMPLeS venue because we were going to see CharLie DiMPLeS . . .

Dad was surprised that I was cross. SO, SO CROSS.

IT'S BECAUSE WE'RE GOING TO SEE CHARLIE DIMPLES!

I shouted. Mum was confused. Why did I point at the advert in the paper if I didn't want to come?

I told her I was pointing at the other advert, OF COURSE. The cool advert. The **X-WING** advert!

Now it was Dad's turn to be confused. If I didn't like CHARLIE DIMPLES, then how come I knew all the words to 'MY SQUISHY WISHY'? I explained that it was all **ELLIE**'s fault and then Mum told me off for picking on her! The only person smiling was **ELLIE**. She got exactly what she wanted and she doesn't even have a magic diary.

I wasn't allowed to stay in the car on my own so I joined my parents and two thousand screaming six-year-old girls at the show.

The next hour and a half was the longest hour and a half of my life. It would have been bad enough watching a

CHARLIE DIMPLES concert anyway, but knowing you're missing an **X-WING** gig at the same time made it doubly bad. We heard all his greatest hits:

1. 'SPRINKLES ON YOUR CUPCAKE'

2. 'GIGGLE MONKEY'

3. 'CHIHUAHUA HOO-HA!'

And then finally it was time for **'MY SQUISHY WISHY'**, which I was kind of relieved about. It meant the concert must be nearly over. The only good thing about all of this — and believe me, it was a tiny thing — was that none of my friends would be seen dead in a place like this. So no one need ever know I was there. No one.

Just before 'MY SQUISHY WISHY' started CHARLIE DIMPLES came to the front of the stage and the crowd fell silent.

It was so quiet you could hear a mouse fart.

Someone's mobile phone went off. I started to laugh. What a loser! Then I realised it was MY MOBILE PHONE. I felt as if two thousand pairs of eyes were turning to glare at me as I fumbled in my pocket.

ELLIE was looking at me as if I'd just killed CHARLIE DIMPLES live on stage, which, believe me, was something I considered doing halfway through

'Chihuahua Hoo-Ha!'

I hadn't read the manual for the phone —
manuals are for losers — so I pushed a button
that I thought would make it stop ringing.

It didn't. In a blind panic, I pressed every
button at the same time. Suddenly there was
a bright flash and then the phone went quiet.
I might have broken it. At that moment
I didn't care.

Charlie played 'MY SQUISHY WISHY'
twice. I still have NO IDEA what a squishy
wishy actually is. But at least the concert
was over.

Back at home I came straight up here to
my bedroom. This day has been a complete
disaster! I thought about changing it all in
this diary, somehow making it so that I went

to **X-WING** after all. But what would be the point in that? Whenever I do change anything, I don't remember the new version anyway, only other people do. No matter what I write, I will never remember being at the **X-WING** gig. I'm trying to look on the bright side, though. At least I've got a phone — but even that hasn't made me feel totally happy, because I know it's **JOSH**'s phone really. And now I've got a Charlie Dimples T-shirt. Thanks, Dad. You are sooo funny.

SUNDAY

Well, diary, the less said about today the better. This morning my ears were still ringing from the CHARLIE DIMPLES concert and it was not helped by **ELLIE** singing all the songs into a hairbrush, one after the other, at the top of her voice.

Even Penelope Fuzzyface looked like she'd had enough. But then Penelope Fuzzyface always looks like she's had enough.

I managed to persuade **ELLIE** to put down the hairbrush and play me at **DEATH SQUADRON**. But something terrible had happened — she was brilliant. She beat me sixteen times in a row.

At first I didn't know what was going on, but then I remembered what I'd written in the diary yesterday. I said that I should have taught her how to play properly. It turned out I did, according to the diary. Thanks for nothing, pal.

By lunchtime I was fed up with being smashed into pixels by my sister so I went to the park for a breath of fresh air. I saw **BRAD RADLEY** coming down the street and tried to hide, but somehow **BRAD** spotted me.

He came up and waved his phone in my face. But for once I didn't care. I had a phone too! In fact, I had the same phone. I took mine out and waved it right back.

But that's not what **BRAD** was trying to tell me.

He clicked a button and my face filled the screen. It was a picture of me at the ChaRLiE DiMPLeS concert and I seemed to be screaming like a girl. What?

BRAD pointed at the buttons on my phone. When I'd mashed them last night to stop it ringing I must have accidentally sent a picture of me at the ChaRLiE DiMPLeS concert to

. . . EVERYONE IN MY CONTACTS LIST!

As this was sinking in, **BRAD** started to boast about how amazing the *X-WING* concert was.

I didn't want to hear any more so I came home. Normally I'd go and talk to **JOSH** about something like this, but he didn't want to see me.

Everything has gone wrong. I've lost my best friend and sent the rest of the school a picture of me at a CHARLIE DIMPLES concert. The phone has ruined my life before I've even made one call. What's more, I didn't get to see *X-WING* in concert and my six-year-old sister can now thrash me on my favourite Xbox game.

I'm sitting here in my bedroom now and trying to think of a way to use this diary to make everything right. Was there something I should have said or something I could have done that would make it all better? But there's nothing I can write to fix this.

This diary has caused me so much trouble. It nearly got me expelled from school and it's cost me my best friend. I should NEVER have used it in the first place. Instead of getting the diary to change things that go wrong, I should be concentrating on making sure things don't go wrong in the first place. And if they do go wrong — as they inevitably will — I need to think about how I can make them better WITHOUT using the diary.

I know exactly where to start . . .

MONDAY

Dear diary, this will be my last ever entry.

This morning I got up early and went to **JOSH**'s house before school.

At first **JOSH** didn't want to see me. But then his mum told him to 'Stop being so silly'. Which we all know is mum-speak for 'Make it up to your buddy.'

Apparently **JOSH** had been moping since we stopped being best friends.

I apologised to him for stealing his idea for the talent show. I admitted that I'd found out about it and decided to copy it — which was true in a way, I just didn't tell him exactly how I'd done it. After a minute or two he was quite nice about it, especially when I gave him the phone to say sorry. Perhaps it's a good thing I don't have a phone. I'm not sure I like phones much anyway. They've made my life a misery these last two weeks.

Just to prove that point, **JOSH** told me he had fixed his phone and someone had sent him the picture of me at the concert. He didn't realise how much I loved ChaRLiE DiMPLeS. I soon realised he was being sarcastic and he started to laugh. He told me that he knew how much I hated Charlie Dimples. He'd guessed ELLIE had wanted me to go, and thought it was really nice of me to take her, especially after she'd helped me win the talent show. He thought that sending a photo like that to everyone showed what a great sense of humour I had.

At first I didn't understand, but then I realised he thought I'd sent the photo on purpose! He thought that it was really cool that I had the confidence to do something like that. Great joke, bro.

I smiled and said, 'I'd do anything for ELLIE, she's one in a million.' Which we all know is Fin-speak for 'She's the most annoying person in the world.'

We were so busy catching up that we didn't notice the time and **JOSH**'s mum ended up driving us to school so we wouldn't be late.

While we were in the car the DJ played the new ***X-WING*** single on the radio and then said how disappointed he'd been that the concert on Saturday night had been cancelled. It's been rescheduled for next week. I couldn't believe my ears! **BRAD** couldn't have seen them on Saturday like he said and I had another chance to see them. Well, I would have if I could find a way into a sold out concert.

In school I made my way to my locker and **BRAD** was waiting for me yet again. He wanted to make the most of the photo I'd sent.

214

Everybody seemed to be there when he started to rub it in, saying that the cool kids like him went to **X-WING** not **Charlie Dimples**.

But I told him that at least my gig had existed! How could he have gone to a show that was cancelled at the last minute? Then, remembering what **JOSH** had thought, I decided to turn the tables. 'Don't you realise that I sent the photo to everyone on purpose?' I said. 'It was supposed to be a joke — as if I'd ever choose to go to a **Charlie Dimples** concert! I was taking the mickey out of myself. Everyone else seemed to get it but you. What's the matter, **BRAD**? No sense of humour?'

It seemed to work! The other kids started

to laugh and **BRAD** suddenly needed to go to the toilet. NOW HE KNEW HOW I FELT.

Then **CLAUDIA RONSON** made her way over and I started to sweat. She said that she wanted to tell me how cool I was. She said it was nice to meet a boy who was 'in touch with his sensitive side', whatever that is. She was fed up with boys talking about **X-WING** all the time. She said she really liked the kind of boy who wrote poetry for his gran and took his little sister to music concerts and even dressed up like CHARLIE DIMPLES from time to time to keep his sister and her friends entertained.

I was too shocked to say anything, but before I knew it, she was asking me out. YES!

216

You read right! **CLAUDIA** asked ME out! We're meeting in town next Saturday.

I didn't care what happened for the rest of the day. For all I knew the school had burned down or been invaded by alien monkeys . . . because I was floating on a cloud made by **CLAUDIA RONSON**. THE WEDDING IS BACK ON!

JOSH and I went back to my house to play Xbox after school, and **JOSH** said he'd been thinking. That was usually something to get worried about, but this time he actually had a good idea. As his parents had got his old phone fixed, he thought we should sell the one I won in the talent show and try to buy two tickets for the rescheduled **X-WING**

concert. The boy is a genius! I knew we were best friends for a reason.

But then it got even better when I came home. It turned out we didn't have to sell anything after all. One of my dad's mates had tickets for the concert but couldn't go to the new show. Dad had bought them off him! I've always said my dad is the best dad ever!

When I got to bed I thought about my day and wondered if there was anything I should change in this diary. **BRAD** was off my back because I'd stood up to him. **JOSH** and I were friends again because I'd said sorry. I was going to see *X-WING* because I had parents who were always thinking about me. And **CLAUDIA RONSON** had asked me out. None of this was thanks to the diary. It was all thanks to ME.

I've realised I don't need a magic diary to make things better, I just need to be myself. If I do the right thing at the right time, I won't have to change it afterwards and if I don't do the right thing at the right time — well, I should do my best to correct mistakes myself. I think it's time to ditch this thing.

Like I said at the start, I'm not a diary person. I'm a STUNTBOY. I don't need a diary like this. It's time to say goodbye. If I want to make millions selling my story in years to come, I'll just have to try and remember it. Meddling with the past like this just isn't worth it. Unless it's something really important. NO! Not even then. This is **FIN SPENCER**: Stuntboy signing off forever.

Although . . . maybe first I should do something about **Ellie** being better than me at **DEATH SQUADRON**. We can't have that, can we?

**Can FIN resist temptation and keep
the diary closed forever?**

Find out more in

ISBN: 978 -1- 84812-447-9

Out now!

Thank you for choosing a Piccadilly Press book.

If you would like to know more about our authors, our books or if you'd just like to know what we're up to, you can find us online.

www.piccadillypress.co.uk

You can also find us on:

We hope to see you soon!